Happy Birthday Nathan!

Boogie On!

FROM:

R J :)

You Got A Boogie

**By
DJ Corchin**

**Illustrated By
Dan Dougherty**

The phazelFOZ Company, LLC

YOU GOT A BOOGIE
Copyright © 2010 By The phazelFOZ Company, LLC.

Published by The phazelFOZ Company, LLC.
Chicago, IL
www.phazelfoz.com
Printed in Taiwan

Library of Congress Number 2010903598

ISBN 978-0-9819645-2-2 (Hardcover)

      978-0-9819645-3-9 (Paperback)

To Scott

My friend has a boogie.

It's quite clear he doesn't know.

I wonder if I should tell him.

My teacher had a boogie once.

My sister had a boogie on her wedding day.

The pictures didn't turn out so well.

The famous chef Pierre had a boogie.

The pitcher had a boogie.

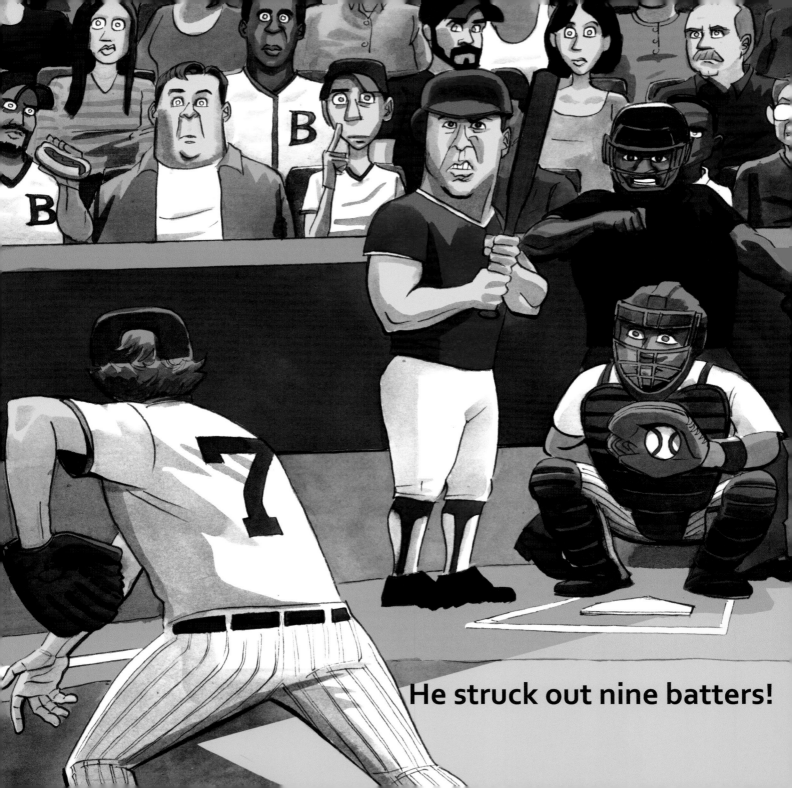

He struck out nine batters!

The ship's captain had a boogie.

She made it all the way to Australia.

My dentist had a boogie.

My dog had a boogie.

And then he didn't.

The dancer had a boogie.

Not the fun kind of boogie.

This kind.

The fireman had a boogie.

I got all wet.

Lots of people get boogies.

That's why friends are so important.

My friend still has a boogie.

I'll tell him because I care.

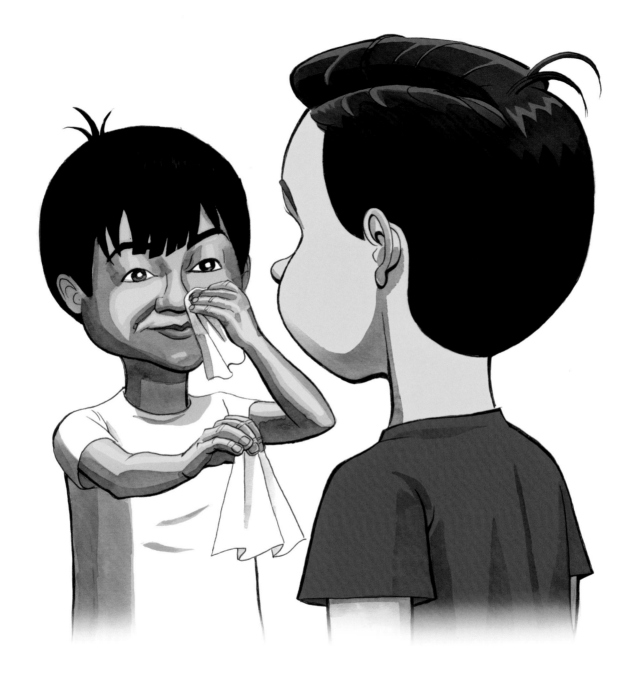

If I had a boogie in my nose…

I'd want to know it's there!

The End

Special thanks to:

Jessica
Scott
Mom
Dan Dougherty
Mike Hurley
Tamara Nolte
Jason Wick

Boogie On

the
phazel**Foz**
company, llc